Stan and Mabel

Beep beep! Beep beep! Beep beep! Beep beep! Beep...

...Beep beep! Beep beep! Beep click!

Yeah? Wha... Oh Mabel! Oh nooo! We've slept in AND I've forgotten my words.
Here's the script. Quick, it's about to start...
SM1

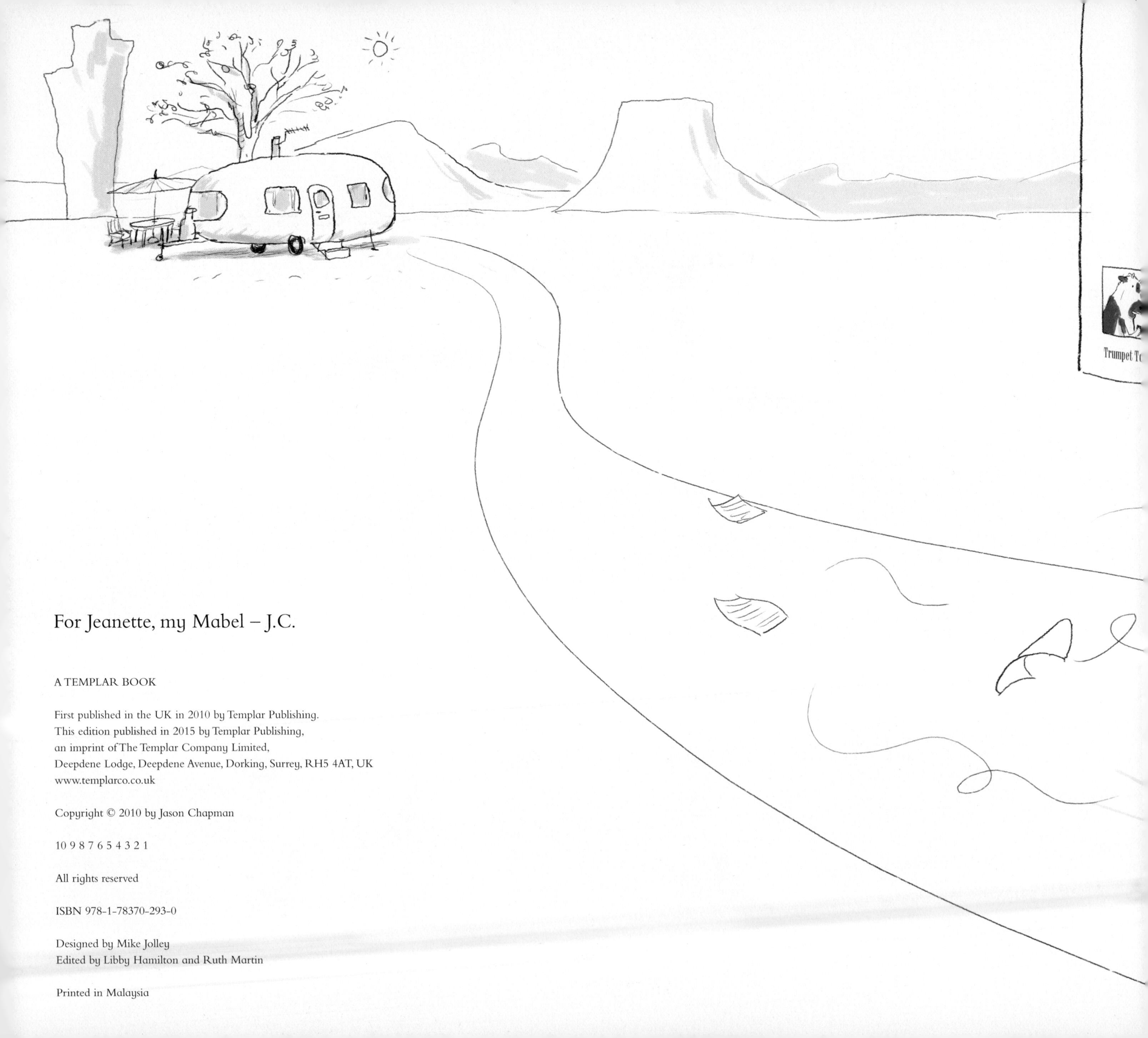

For Jeanette, my Mabel – J.C.

A TEMPLAR BOOK

First published in the UK in 2010 by Templar Publishing.
This edition published in 2015 by Templar Publishing,
an imprint of The Templar Company Limited,
Deepdene Lodge, Deepdene Avenue, Dorking, Surrey, RH5 4AT, UK
www.templarco.co.uk

Copyright © 2010 by Jason Chapman

10 9 8 7 6 5 4 3 2 1

All rights reserved

ISBN 978-1-78370-293-0

Designed by Mike Jolley
Edited by Libby Hamilton and Ruth Martin

Printed in Malaysia

Templar Publishing Presents

Stan and Mabel

A STORY BY
JASON CHAPMAN

INTRODUCING

templar publishing

This is a story about a dog called Stan and a cat called Mabel.
They live all the way up here.

Oops! No, that's not them,
that's Lulu the donkey.
They must live here.

Sorry, Deirdre Duck.
Maybe here?

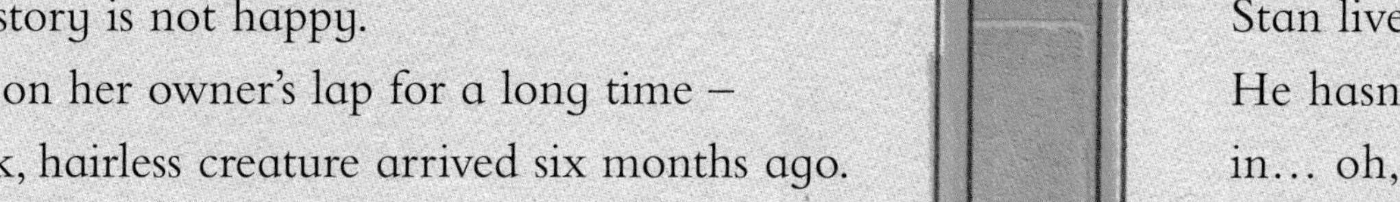

The start of our story is not happy.
Mabel hasn't sat on her owner's lap for a long time – not since the pink, hairless creature arrived six months ago.

Stan lives next door.
He hasn't been out for a walk in the park in… oh, ever so long.

One thing that makes them both happy is when the lady downstairs plays her beautiful music.

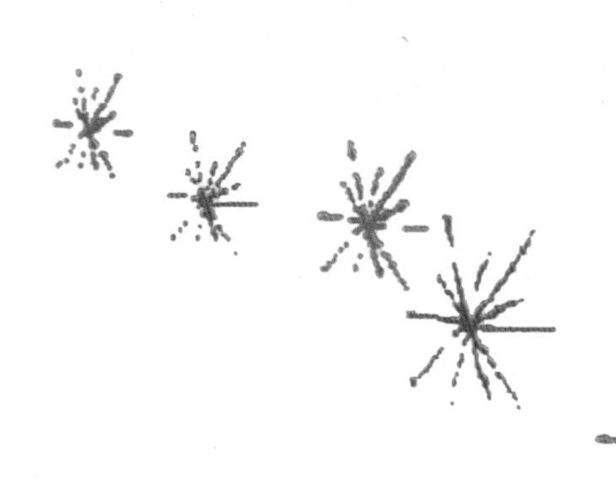

But one day the music lady went away.
Days went by – days and days without music.

"Stanley, it's Mabel. I can't take it any longer. We need to get out of here... and we need to do it tonight."

“T-t-tonight?” said Stan.
“B-b-but I haven’t packed my things.”
“Get packing,” said Mabel, “because tonight’s the ni… Ow-ow-ow!
Get off my tail!”

As Stan hurriedly packed his bowl and brush into a case, he heard a tap at the window. It was Mabel on the other side… ten floors up.

“Mabel! That’s dangerous,” said Stan, opening the window. Unfortunately, Stan had forgotten that his window opened outwards, and he knocked Mabel off the window ledge…

but he managed to grab her tail just in time.

Hanging upside down, Mabel looked straight into the music lady's flat and had what artists call 'a flash of inspiration'.

"Bingo!" said Mabel, reading a poster stuck up on the wall.
"Pull me up, Stanley."
"Are you alright, Mabel?" asked Stan sheepishly.
"Never better, Stanley. I've got an idea. Quick, let's go. And bring that banjo of yours – the one you play when your owner goes out."

They ran and they ran. It seemed like the city would never end.

"Where are we going?" panted Stan, as he stopped to catch his breath. "And why the banjo?"

"The music lady…" puffed Mabel, "she's gone to Italy – to a competition to find the Greatest Orchestra in the World. I saw the poster through her window. And the banjo? Well, we're auditioning too!"

"Mabel, you're mad," sighed Stan.

As they crossed the bridge to leave the city, they met a duck called Roady.

"Where are you going?" asked Roady.

"We're going to Italy," said Stan.

"To audition in a competition to find the Greatest Orchestra in the World," added Mabel.

"Can I come too?" asked Roady. "I'm an oboe virtuoso."

"Of course you may," said Mabel, with delight.

Walking through the suburbs, Stan, Mabel and Roady heard a strange sound: thumpety-thump-thump... thumpety-thump-thump.

They followed the noise into someone's garden, and found two rabbits making the most amazing racket.

"I like the beat of your feet," said Mabel.
"Thanks," said one of the rabbits. "I'm Roberta, and this is Bobby."

"Nice to meet you," said Roady, "would you like to join our orchestra? We're going to Italy to play in a competition and we could really use a couple of good drummers."

"Sure!" said Roberta, and she invited them to sleep over at her house.

The next morning, Stan, Mabel, Roady, Bobby and Roberta met a horse called Houston. He was carrying a bassoon.

"Where are you all going?" asked Houston.
"We're an orchestra, on our way to Italy," said Roberta. "We're going to enter a competition to find the Greatest Orchestra in the World. Would you like to join us?"
"That sounds great," said Houston. "I can play my bassoon."

As they passed a farm, they met a herd of cows.

"Hello, cows," said Houston. "We're going to Italy to audition in a competition to find the Greatest Orchestra in the World, but we are a few members short. I don't suppose you know anyone who might care to join us, do you?"

"My dear! It's your lucky day," said Margaret the cow.
"We all play instruments. We'll just have to pop to the music shop to pick them up. They're being cleaned and restrung, you see – you have no idea how dirty they get when you play them in a field."

Then they all took a short taxi trip
to the bus station...

caught a bus to the train station...

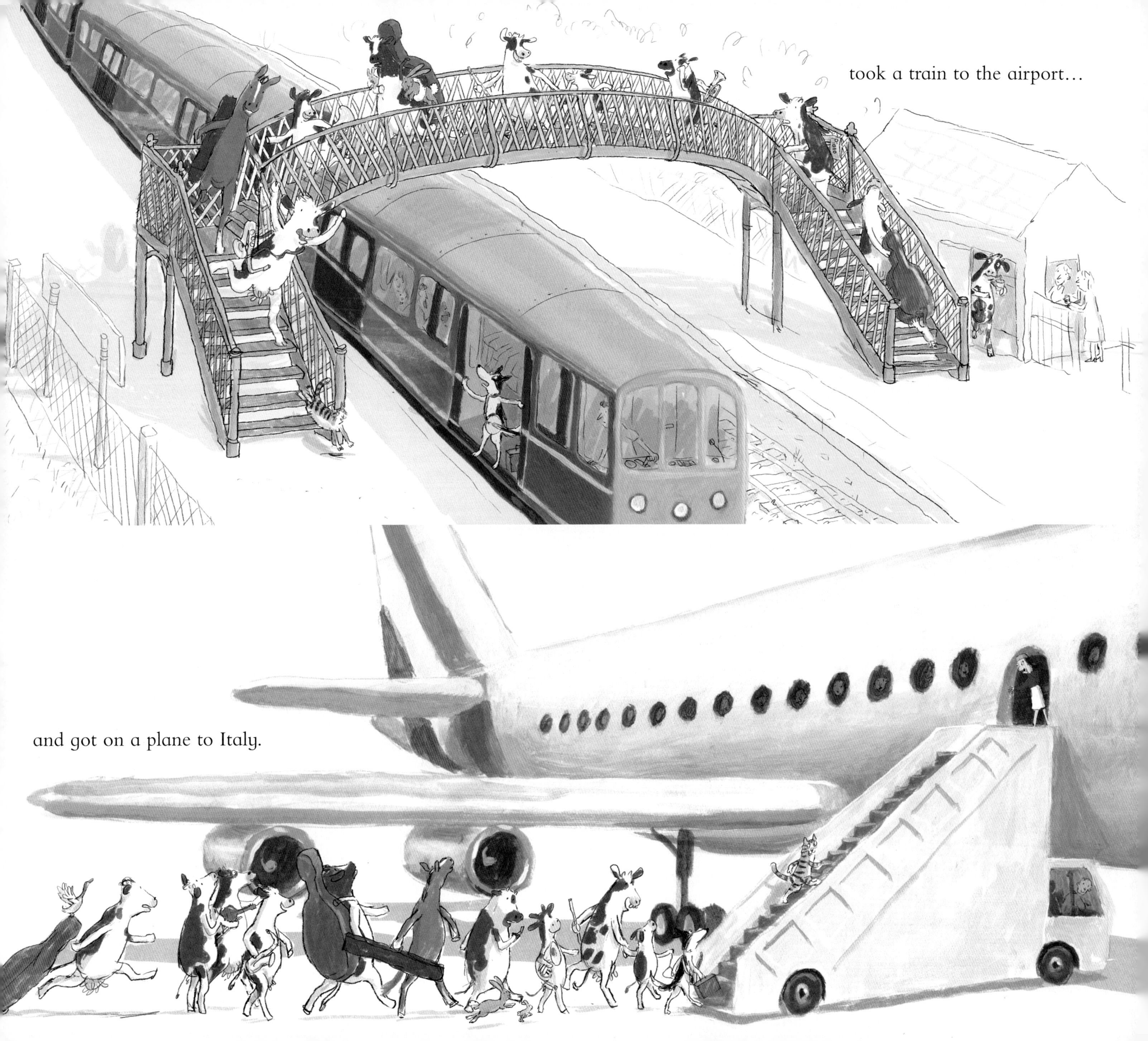

took a train to the airport…

and got on a plane to Italy.

After a long flight, they arrived at Milan airport just as the sun was setting.

For some, the nerves were beginning to show.

A short walk took them to the magnificent La Scala opera house, where they found a long, long queue of musicians wanting to take part in the competition to find the Greatest Orchestra in the World.

After a long wait, it was the turn of Stan, Mabel and their friends to impress the judges. As they walked onto the stage and raised their instruments, a hush fell over the whole audience.

But as soon as they began to play, the animals made an awful racket, because, of course, animals can't play instruments!

Several judges covered their ears and one even booed.

Sad and dejected, the animals left the stage, their dreams in tatters.

They were about to go home, when one of the judges came running after them. It was the music lady from downstairs!

She called the animals back to the hall and turned to the judges.
“Esteemed judges of La Scala, I think we have overlooked some unusual talent here. I give you… the Greatest Animal Orchestra in the World.”

After a silence that felt like forever, one judge slowly stood up and began to clap… and then so did another… and another… until the whole crowd stood on their feet applauding.

Within a week, they had begun a world tour!
"We did it," said Stan. "We only went and did it."
"This, my dear Stanley, is just the beginning," said Mabel.

And it was…

THE GREATEST
ANIMAL ORCHESTRA
IN THE WORLD
ROYAL ALBERT HALL

DOG
SHAM
POO

STAGE
MABEL
Ooh! Look here: 'Stan and Mabel hit the big time with a moo-ving performance.'